Soccer Girl
Takes the Kick

By Julie Chadwick

Copyright © 2014 Julie Chadwick

Edited by Rob Chadwick

Cover by Julie Chadwick, Olivia Chadwick, Madelyn Chadwick, and Katie Chadwick

ISBN:1505323525
ISBN-13: 978-1505323528

DEDICATION

For my sweet daughters Madelyn, Katie and Olivia. You are my favorite soccer girls.

CONTENTS

Chapter 1 - Josie

My name is Josie Howard. I am ten years old and in fourth grade. My best friends call me Jose. I like being a fourth grader because we are the oldest class in the elementary school. We rule the school!   Most of the other kids either look up to us or are scared of us. There is really nothing to be scared of, but still I like having that power!

I have two sisters, an older sister and a younger sister. It stinks being the middle sister. My older sister's name is Ellie, and she is in seventh grade. She gets to do everything. She even has her own phone. She never lets me use it. It's not fair. I even have to wear all her old clothes, and she likes to buy everything that has sparkles on it. I hate sparkles! She is so girlie with her pink and purple. My favorite color is orange. I never get to wear orange. If I could wear anything I wanted, it would be yoga pants and orange t-shirts, not skirts and sparkles. If only, I was born first.

My younger sister is in first grade and her name is Lily. She always cries and gets me in trouble. It wasn't my fault the soccer ball hit her in the face when I kicked it. She should have gotten out of the way. She is so much smaller than me that whenever I play with her, she gets shoved to the ground. I tell my Mom that is was an accident, but I always get in trouble anyways. She gets everything too. She doesn't have to wear any of my old clothes because they usually have holes in them when I grow out of them. She is very girlie too. She is always changing into dresses. You will not catch me wearing a dress!

All of us do have one thing in common. We all love soccer! We play soccer all the time. Ellie never just lets me win. She always makes a point of taking the ball away from me.

It makes me mad! I always lose to her. She is so easy on Lily though. She always lets her score and win. Someday, I want to be as good as Ellie. I practice all the time. I even have a soccer ball pillow that I juggle indoors. One of these days I am going to beat Ellie!

Chapter 2 – When I Was Little

Ever since I was four years old, I played soccer. I remember my Mom always telling me, "Josie, guess what? When you turn four you can play soccer." I wasn't really sure what soccer was, just that when you turn four something magical happens and everybody is supposed to play soccer. So that is what I did. I played soccer!

It turns out that my birthday is at the end of February and spring season starts in March. So we had to practice before the first game and guess when practiced started? The day after my fourth birthday. It was finally happening. I turned four and soccer was finally going to begin.

I remember thinking that soccer was a lot harder than I had thought it was going to be. There is a lot of running involved and I was tired. What was my Mom so excited about?

I could hear my Dad yelling on the side line for me to go get the ball. He should try running for forty minutes straight. I was tired! Half the time I didn't know which direction to run with the ball.

This one time, I accidentally scored in my own goal. It can be confusing, both goals look exactly the same. Maybe they should not paint both goals all white. I think the field should have one blue goal and one orange goal. That way, the adults could yell "Run towards the blue goal!"

You really have to pay attention while you are on the field. My Dad used to say, "Josie, keep your head on a swivel, head on a swivel." What was he talking about and why did he always repeat it twice? "Head on a swivel," what does that even mean? Well, I did figure out what that meant!

One game I was kicking this really pretty patch of green grass with my foot and had my head down. All of a sudden something hit me in the head. I thought, "Hey, who did that? Oh, it was the soccer ball! That hurt!" I really needed to watch where the ball was. I don't want to get hit in the head again.

I still don't know why my Dad had to repeat it twice though. Plus, if he had just said, "Josie watch the ball at all times, you don't want to get hit in the head." Then maybe I would have understood and could have saved myself the pain and embarrassment.

I still remember my first goal. I stole the ball from the green team and started dribbling toward the goal. I could feel my heart beating. I heard a lot of parents yelling, but had no idea what they were saying. I don't understand why parents yell so much. It just sounds like a bunch of muffled noise.

Anyway, I was running toward the goal and made a big kick. It went past the goalie and made a huge swishing sound when it hit the net. I fist pumped both hands into the air and started jumping up and down. My teammates came running at me to give me a hug. They were running so fast I was afraid they were going to knock me over!

That is when my love of soccer began. There is no better feeling than scoring goals. Now I knew what my Mom and Dad were so excited about.

Chapter 3 - Portville

I moved to a small town in
Michigan when I was in first grade.
The town has only one thousand
people in it. It is called Portville.
Portville has this really pretty
lighthouse and sandy beach.

When my Dad told me we were moving to Portville, I was so excited because I thought I was going to live in the lighthouse. Turns out, we moved into a regular house. What a major let down!

It is really cold in Michigan so I don't spend that much time at the beach. Anyway, who has time for the beach when I need to practice my soccer skills? I have a championship to win.

There is a town next to us called Middleton. Portville and Middleton are huge rivals! We play their teams and our own teams during the regular soccer season, but all of our games lead up to winning the championship. Middleton has a huge tournament every year, and the winner gets a gigantic trophy and a team picture in the paper. The winners are practically famous!

Plus it is all the kids talk about in school. Hey Josie, "Think we will win the championship this year?" Hey Josie, "This is going to be your year." Hey Josie, "You are so awesome, you are definitely going to

win the championship this year!"
Okay, so I made up that last part, but people were definitely thinking it.

Since my town is so small, we have both girls and boys on my team. There is not enough girls or boys to make our own team so we have to combine. I like playing with the boys. There is nothing sweeter then scoring on a boy or taking the ball away from him. I remember scoring on John and I heard him say, "Have you ever heard of a girl scoring?" Yes John, girls score all the time!

Every year they make different soccer teams. Some kids you have had on your team before and some are new. The first practice is the most exciting so you can see who is on your team this year. Some kids you are happy about and some kids you are not so happy about. Everyone on my team has one thing in common this year. We are going to win the championship!

Chapter 4 – Getting a Coach

Now that I am in fourth grade, I must win this championship. I will not be in second place again! I have come in second place for three years in a row. Yes, I said three. It is horrible!

My Mom says that I should be proud of second place. Whatever, second place is just second, I want to win. I want to be famous! I can just hear the people chanting my name, "Josie, Josie, Josie!"

My best friend is Emma and she plays soccer too. We have been on the same team for the past three years. That is how we met. The first day of soccer practice she asked me if I wanted to pass with her. I said, "Sure", seeing that I didn't know anyone else since I just moved here. Emma is really good at soccer and really sweet. She bought me a best friend necklace. She gave me the best charm and her the friends charm. It was in the shape of a soccer ball. When you put them together it says best friends. We have been best friends since she gave me that necklace. I accidentally broke the necklace when bouncing on my trampoline, but I was really happy when she gave it to me. I hope Emma is on my team again!

Coaches are not allowed to pick their own players. The soccer director usually places the kids on each team based on their skill level. They try to keep all the teams even. It would not be fair if one team was really good and another team was really bad. This way each player will have a better chance to win the tournament.

I heard the phone ring last night and my Dad was talking. He yelled, "Josie that was your soccer coach. His name is Coach Chad." I have never heard of Coach Chad. "Is he a good coach?" I asked. My Dad says, "I don't know. He said he has never coached before and doesn't really know anything about soccer."

"What!" I yelled. "How am I supposed to win the championship, if he doesn't know anything about soccer?" I yelled some more. This is not good. I just hope Emma's on my team.

Chapter 5 - School

My Mom drives me and my sisters to school every morning. I couldn't wait to get to school this morning. I just know the class is going to be buzzing about who got who for a soccer coach.

Lily is so slow in the morning. She always makes me late to class. "Come on Lily, it is time to go," I yelled. Lily was still eating breakfast and playing games on her Kindle. "Mom, make her go faster, I need to get to school," I said. "Okay honey, Lily is getting ready. You need to calm down, we still have plenty of time," Mom said.

We finally got to school. As I was walking into class I could hear the kids talking about what team they were on. Emma turns to me and says,

"Jose, I got coach Jeff, who did you get?" I felt my stomach drop because Emma wasn't going to be on my team this year. That stinks! I said, "Oh no, I got Coach Chad. Have you heard anyone else say that?" When I saw the huge grin come over her face, I knew this wasn't good. Emma said that she heard Jake talking about getting Coach Chad. This was beyond bad! Jake is so nice and a good friend of mine, but he is more of a gymnast than a soccer player. He is all the time twirling and doing cartwheels during the games.

None of my other friends got Coach Chad. I guess I will have to wait until practice tonight to see who else is on my team. Please, please, please let there be some good kids!

Chapter 6 – First Practice

Tonight is my first practice! I can't wait to meet my coach and see who else besides Jake is on my team. "Come on Mom, it is time to go. I don't want to be late!" I yelled.

We finally get to the soccer fields. I am getting out of the car and I feel a nervous feeling in my belly. I am just so excited. We just have to win the tournament this year! I notice my team at the back field. I can spot Jake doing cartwheels on the field.

My Mom walks me to the field and introduces me to Coach Chad. He is very tall and skinny. He doesn't really look like a soccer player. I hope he is a good coach. I spot my other teammates and breathe a huge sigh of relief. I see Nate and Liv waving to me. They are both awesome players. There are a few kids that I don't know because they go to the private school in town, but they look like they might be good. I am starting to feel hopeful again.

Coach Chad introduces all the kids to each other. So there is me, Jake, Nate, Liv, Cole, Nick, Kate, and Maddie. There is four girls and four boys on the team. He starts talking about himself. Wait! What? Did he just say he really doesn't know anything about soccer? That he is going to need our help figuring this out? Oh no! My hopefulness that I was starting to feel earlier is disappearing.

Practice lasted for an hour and it actually went pretty well. It was kind of obvious that Coach Chad has no idea what he is doing, but luckily most of the kids on my team have played before. I am starting to feel good about the team again. Coach Chad passed out the uniforms and told us we needed to come up with a name for the team, while he spoke with the parents.

Our uniforms were bright orange. I told my teammates, "Guys, I have the best name. How about Orange Crush?" Some grumbled and didn't like it. "Come on. Please! That is an awesome name. I will bring everyone Orange Crush to the tournament," I said. They all decided that Orange Crush was a great name. There is nothing that bribing with a little soda can't fix.

I was able to get the number 20. Twenty is my favorite number because that is Abby Wambach's number on the Women's USA Soccer team.   She is awesome! I think I play a lot like she does or maybe how she must have played when she was in the fourth grade. I hope someday I can head in a bunch of goals too!

Coach Chad explained to our parents that our first game is this Thursday. This is just a regular game against another team in Portville. We play six games in Portville and then the last weekend is the Middleton tournament.

Just hearing the words Middleton tournament got all the kids talking. "We are going to be the champions this year!" Nate said. "Yeah, we are going to win this year," said Liv. I agreed. "I cannot come in second again!" I said.

Chapter 7 - Orange Crush's First Game

Our first game is tonight at 6 o'clock. We are playing Emma's team. This could be bad. She told me she had Kyle on her team. He is so good.

My Mom made spaghetti with meatballs for dinner. She is not really a very good cook, but I usually like her spaghetti. Tonight I am feeling too nervous to eat.

It is finally time for the game so we drive over to the fields. I walk to the field. I see Emma and wave to her. Her team is bright green and they look like they know what they are doing. Their coach has them warming up with drills. My team is sitting on top of their soccer balls laughing and talking to each other.

Coach Chad comes over to talk to us and tells us our position. I am starting at offense. He also told Jake that he was the goalie. I am wondering if that is really a very good idea, but he is the coach.

We got to kick off with the ball and I dribbled around everyone and scored the first goal. That is the last goal that we scored. Emma's team beat us 5 to 1. It was not pretty. We have a lot of work to do if we are going to win the tournament this year. Right now, I am wondering if we are going to win a game.

Chapter 8 – Orange Crush Wins a Game

So far we have lost against every team in Portville. We have lost five straight games. We are officially the worst team in town!

Coach Chad always says that it doesn't matter if we win or lose. All that matters is that we are having fun. Hmm, I don't think anyone thinks losing is very fun! I heard him tell our parents that the kids don't really keep track of the score, that we are just having a blast and improving our skills. I think to myself, I am ten years old and I know how to count.

It would be nice if we could win tonight. We are playing against the red Portville team. I have heard that they are not very good, so maybe we have a chance. This is the last regular game before the Middleton tournament next weekend.

I don't know what was going on during the game but Nate, Liv and I were on fire! Nate scored two goals. Liv kept stealing the ball and dribbling down the field. She would cross to me in the middle and I would kick it in. I even tried to head the ball in but I completely missed it. It was a little embarrassing!

Maddie and Kate played awesome defense. They were like a brick wall. No one could get past them. This was lucky because Jake was in goal doing handstands again. Even Nick and Cole were making great passes. We actually won the game 6 to 0!

Orange Crush was finally coming together. If we play like we played tonight, we may have a chance next weekend at the Middleton tournament!

Chapter 9 – Getting Ready for Middleton

I woke up this morning at 7 o'clock, and I am buzzing with excitement. The Middleton tournament is finally here and I can't wait to win that trophy and become famous!

I got dressed in my orange uniform and started jumping up and down on my bed. It is time for Orange Crush to show the town that we are champions!

I ate my breakfast quickly and yelled at my family to get moving. My first game is at 9 o'clock and I can't be late. I tell Lily to go get ready since she is always so slow. I don't want to be late. Ellie's team is also in the tournament so she is ready to go.

I grabbed the Orange Crush soda from the refrigerator and put it in the car. I had promised my team I would bring it to the tournament if they let us go by that awesome name. Before each game, we huddle into a circle and put one hand in, then we yell, "Orange Crush will crush you!"

I arrive at the field thirty minutes early. Some of the games have already started. I find some of my friends and their parents. My parents brought a lot of snacks with them, since I plan to be here all day.

This tournament is a double elimination, which means we have to lose twice in order to be out of the tournament. Some teams lose two games in a row and go home. If my team keeps winning, we get to come back tomorrow for the championship game.

I can feel the excitement in the air. I spot Coach Chad and notice some of my teammates sitting around and talking and laughing on their soccer ball again. I walk up to them and say, "Come on guys, no sitting on balls, we need to get our head in the game. Let's go warm up. We have a tournament to win." Maddie mumbles, "Calm down Josie."

Coach Chad has us huddle around to tell us the tournament schedule. If we win four games today, we will be in the championship game tomorrow. We are playing two Middleton teams and two Portville teams, unless we lose twice and then we are out of the tournament. I mumble to myself, "That better not happen."

Chapter 10 – The Games Begin

The first team we played was against the worst Middleton team in the league. It seems like the Middleton teams are either really good or really bad. Luckily, we played against the worst team first. This should give us some confidence.

Emma came to watch me play. I scored three goals. We won the first game 4 to 0.

Orange Crush was off to a good start. Our next game was in an hour, so I watched Emma play her game. Emma scored two goals and they also won. Her team is really good and may be our main competition. I really wish Emma was on my team. We would have been unstoppable.

We win our next two games. We win 1 to 0 and 3 to 1. We are feeling on top of the world! We only have one more game to win today and we will be in the championship game! Go Orange Crush!

It is time for our last game today. We have to play against the really good Middleton team. I called my team into a huddle. "Guys, we need everyone to be on fire this game. We have to beat these guys. Everyone needs to be first to the ball." I see Kate rolling her eyes at me. She mumbles, "Josie, you know you aren't our coach, right?"

Coach Chad comes over to tell us to have fun. He gives everyone their positions. I am starting at offense. I feel butterflies in my stomach.

The Middleton team gets the ball first. They dribble down the field and score immediately. What just happened? We are already losing and the game just started.

I kick the ball to Nate and we dribble down the field. We don't make it very far before a Middleton player takes the ball away. This may be a long game.

It is halftime and we are still losing 0 to 1. Our defense started playing better after that first goal was scored against us. Maddie has saved so many possible goals. She is playing awesome today.

Coach Chad tells us to sip some water and that we are playing great. He says, "Just go out there and have a great time. Don't worry about the score." I am definitely worried.

The second half of the game has been really hard. Both teams have been going after the ball. I know that the buzzer is going to sound soon to signal that the game is over. We are still losing 0 to 1. I am starting to feel frantic.

I heard my Dad on the sidelines yell, "Josie, five minutes!" This gives me extra energy. I get first to the ball and start running down the field. I make a move around the defender and keep dribbling.

I can hear so much noise. Parents yelling for me to go. The goalie comes charging at me. I can feel my heart racing. Out of the corner of my eye, I notice that Liv is wide open. I pass it by the goalie, who is still charging at me. It feels like everything is moving in slow motion. The ball goes right in front of the goal and I see Liv sprinting towards it. Liv gets to the ball and shoots it into the goal. It was beautiful!

I fist pump both my fists into the air and start running to Liv. I give her a high five. We are now tied 1 to 1 with probably three minutes to go. If we tie, we have to do five penalty kicks. Whoever gets the most kicks in wins the game. I would rather not have it go to penalty kicks.

The Middleton team lines up for the kickoff. I hear my Dad yelling that we have two minutes left. I steal the ball away from the Middleton team and pass it to Nate. He dribbles down the field and kicks it. It hits their defender in the hand while in the goalie box. The referee calls a hand ball and it is a free kick. Coach Chad yells for Nate to take it.

I walk over to Nate and give him a fist pump. I say, "Nate you got this. Kick it to the open space." Nate is left footed so I am a little worried about the kick. Sometimes his kick curves to the left and completely misses the goal. Nate steps back and kicks the ball to the left corner. The goalie dives in the air but misses it. Nate scored! We all start jumping up and down.

The buzzer sounds and we win the game 2 to 1. That was a close one. We made it to the championship game! Coach Chad calls us into a huddle. He says, "Great jobs guys. Get some rest tonight and I will see you tomorrow at 10 o'clock for the championship game." We all start chanting. "Orange Crush, Orange Crush, Orange Crush."

I go and find Emma to tell her the good news and see how her team is doing. We may have to play them tomorrow. Emma tells me that her team and the Middleton team each have one loss. They have to play each other to see which team will be in the championship game against us tomorrow.

Emma is going to call me later and tell me how it went. I wished her luck and find my family to go home. My legs feel like jelly. Playing four soccer games in one day is exhausting.

Chapter 11 – Championship Game

I talked to Emma last night and they lost to the Middleton team in a penalty shoot-out. She tells me that we have to win for Portville since we are the last team that hasn't been eliminated. Orange Crush must take down Middleton!

They have already lost once. If we win this game we are the champions. If we lose, we have to play them again. Each team must lose twice to be eliminated.

I am so pumped up, I can't wait. I am walking out to the field and I spot my team right away. I sigh and roll my eyes. The other team is warming up and my team is sitting on their soccer balls laughing again. I start clapping my hands getting their attention. "Come on guys, we need to warm up!" I yell.

Coach Chad tells us how proud of us he is. "Go out there and try your hardest," he says. He tells us our positions and we line up. I am starting at offense again. Jake is starting as goalie. This is not good!

Things do not go well during this game. Jake let in three goals. One went right through his legs. The whole team seemed very sleepy. We lose 0 to 3.

I am very concerned! Each team now has one loss and we have to play each other again. Whoever wins this game, wins the championship! I cannot come in second four years in a row! I hate second!

The second game is about to start and I call my team into a huddle. "Orange Crush, we can do this! We need big shots, good passes, and be first to the ball," I say. We all put our hand in and yell, "Orange Crush will crush you!"

Coach Chad tells us our positions and mumbles something about having a blast. We line up and start the game.

This is an exhausting game. Both teams are playing awesome. Neither one of us can make anything happen. Every time I try to make a run the Middleton team is right there taking it away. The score is still 0 to 0.

I hear my Dad yell that we only have four minutes left. The Middleton team has the ball going for a break away. I notice that Jake is in goal. This is not good. I run as fast as I can to get back there. I can feel my heart pounding and my legs are burning. I am almost there. The

Middleton boy swings his leg back for the shot. I can't quite make it there in time so I decide to slide and kick the ball. I made it to the ball just in time and kick it out of bounds. I hear the parents screaming, "Great job Josie!"

That was a close one. We only have two minutes left in the game. Maddie stops the ball and kicks it up to Liv. Liv runs it up the sideline and crosses it to the middle. Nate and I are sprinting to the middle of the goal. I hear the buzzer sound in the background to signal that the game is over. I get to the ball and kick it into the goal! I fist pump both hands into the air and start jumping up and down. My team is yelling and jumping up and down.

The referee starts blowing his whistle and starts yelling, "No goal, no goal. The buzzer sounded before the goal was shot. It doesn't count." I do remember hearing the buzzer in the background. Oh no, this means we have to go to a penalty shoot-out!

Coach Chad calls us over so he can tell us who will be the five kickers. He says, "Nate, I want you to be the goalie." I breathe a sigh of relief that he didn't put Jake or myself in goal. I get really nervous when I have to play goalie. Coach Chad says, "The kickers are Maddie, Josie, Liv, Nate, and Kate."

Each team takes turn kicking the penalty kick. The Middleton team is kicking first. They have their best kicker go first. He backs up and makes a beautiful kick to the top left corner. There was no way Nate could get to that ball. I yell, "It is okay Nate, don't worry about it."

Nate takes our first kick and kicks it low in the bottom left corner. It is tied 1 to 1. Nate goes back into goal and stops the next shot. We all start jumping up and down screaming. Kate takes our next kick and kicks it over the goal posts. It is still tied 1 to 1.

Middleton's next two kickers make their shots. Maddie and Liv both make our shots. It is tied 3 to 3. The last Middleton kicker is about to go. He winds up and kicks it towards the left. Nate dives and pushes the ball out of bounds. He missed the shot!

I am taking the last shot. The championship is all up to me. If I make my shot, we win the big trophy! I am so scared I can hardly feel my legs. I take two steps back from the ball and one to the left. I am lined up perfectly. I see the goalie's eyes trying to stare me down. I will not be intimidated!

I decide I am going to kick the ball to the top left corner. I am looking right hoping to fake the goalie out. I move forward and take the shot. The ball soars through the air into the top left corner. I can hear the swishing of the net. My team starts jumping up and down screaming! We won! We won! We finally won the Middleton tournament!

We make our way over to the tent to collect that gigantic trophy and get our picture taken! The trophy is the most beautiful thing I have ever seen. It is gold with a huge soccer ball on top and at the bottom it spells out CHAMPIONS! I have never been so happy in my life! My smile is so big it almost hurts. We are going to be famous!

ABOUT THE AUTHOR

Julie H. Chadwick graduated from the University of Kentucky with a degree in Chemical Engineering. She worked as a Chemical Engineer for many years. She decided to stay home after having her daughters. Julie grew up playing soccer and loves watching her daughters play. This book was inspired by watching many games. Julie loves to read and write during her free time. She also wrote <u>Suzie Makes the Move and Swishes the Shot</u>. She lives with her family in Zionsville, Indiana.

11143666R00043

Printed in Great Britain
by Amazon